Kissing the Coronavirus 3: The Mutant Strain

M.J. Edwards

They say the new strain is resistant to

vaccines, but is it resistant to sex?

For Chump
My beautiful boy

Dr Amy Amyson couldn't stop thinking about the incredible sex she'd partaken in not twelve hours before. It was like the entire four-and-a-half-minute act was permanently lodged in her temporal lobe, which is the part of the brain that stores your memories — amazing sexual encounters included. Dr Amyson knew that, because she was a microbiologist, and so had all sorts of intricate medical knowledge.

Something else she couldn't stop thinking about was the positive Covid-19 test she had received just ten minutes after that erotically charged moment. She hoped and prayed that she hadn't unwittingly spread the virus to others. She was usually so careful. Blast her inability to control her vagina!

Dr Amyson's most recent climatic encounter — which, as mentioned a few sentences back, was half a day ago — had been something to behold. Something to behold indeed.

Just the thought of it sent her vagina spinning like a thing that spins a lot. She pummeled at her own breast and chomped on her lips and her bum quivered at the mere thought of what had happened. She was sitting in her chair, in the middle of the laboratory canteen, but it was four in the morning so there was nobody around to see. Besides, even if there was, it would have simply added to the cheekiness that made her pussy so wet it was like a sunburnt sea lion fresh out of the ocean. Even her positive Covid-19 test couldn't dampen her sexual spirits.

Pity she was alone. The sheer memory was enough to send an orgasm rippling through her body like her vagina had been filled with bees.

Start of flashback

Dr Amyson sat on the 2:52 flight from Finland to North Virginia, on her way back from the annual microbiology convention which was so critical to her microbiological work. She had spent three whole days discussing the latest microbiological breakthroughs centred around the Coronavirus pandemic (there were several) with colleagues from all across the world, including Professor Theon Wallbreaker, Denmark's leading micro-biomedical researcher (who she sucked off in a storage cupboard, but this flashback isn't about him) and Sir Rogerson Tilbert (who she tried to suck off but he is very old so he couldn't become engorged — but this flashback isn't about him either).

It was a who's who of celebrities from the microbiological world, which would often just end in science-fueled sex sessions because it was the one and only time in the microbiology calendar where people who understood the human anatomy inside (literally) and out (literally) got together. When the learning was done, it was time to put that knowledge into practice — via sex.

But surprisingly, despite the world's top microbiologists being on hand to teach Dr Amyson things about her body even she was yet to discover, it was not during the convention where she experienced her knee-knockingly-world-shatteringly-perception-altering orgasm.

No.

It was on that 2:52 flight from Finland to North Virginia.

Dr Amyson sat watching her favourite movie, *Big Momma's House 2*, on the TV monitor on the back of the seat in front. She sipped a glass of Monet and ate some nuts, wishing they were another sort of nut she could be chewing instead (hehe). The deep red wine made her lips blush burgundy, which matched the skirt of the air hostess who handed her another bottle of wine. Wait, did she wink? Dr Amyson was sure she did.

Dr Amyson wondered if her vagina was the same inviting shade as her skirt...

Phew, she thought. Her sexual frustration was getting the better of her.

It had been two years since the coronavirus pandemic had first snatched the lives and freedoms away from so many people across the world — and ruined Dr Amyson's sex life — with wave after wave striking every few months. Lockdowns came and went, businesses closed and reopened, and that was the only time Dr Amyson was free to enjoy as much mucky sex fun time as she could handle — and she could handle a lot, which was why it was so frustrating. And she didn't mind *what* she handled, nor on whom. She was happy with a dick clumsily fucking her soapy tits like an eager boy scout cleaning a car windscreen with a slab of chorizo, a vagina rubbing gently against her forearm like a chewed beefburger, or anything in between. She just loved genitals. She loved touching genitals, kissing genitals, and putting things inside her own — and of course other people's — genitals.

The sexual misadventures that had taken place during the microbiology convention were plaguing Dr Amyson's grey matter, which is what she and her microbiology colleagues knew as the brain. Sure, she had been throat-punched by two of the industry's biggest names (even if they weren't the *biggest,* she thought with a chuckling chuckle) but overall, the convention hadn't been as fruitful as it had been years before. There was a new Covid variation emerging in Scandinavia called the D1K strain, which had been given the amusing nickname of *the dick strain.* Apparently, it was resistant to vaccines, and sat dormant in your system for twelve hours before releasing the infection into your cells, so the con-goers were understandably far more concerned about wearing masks and using hand sanitiser than getting their genitals wet.

Usually, during the flight home from Finland, Dr Amyson would have to book two seats so she could sit legs akimbo and air out her vagina, which would be aching from all the hot sex she'd had, but this year she only required one seat. Sure, she had learned a lot about the pandemic, and how microbiologists were doing their part to help keep new mutations of the virus at bay, but what she'd really wanted to come away from the convention with was a feeling of sexual satisfaction that only came from an immeasurable amount of genitalia hitting, tickling or gouging you in any one of your five orifices, which were what microbiologists like Dr Amyson called *holes*.

It was no good.

Dr Amyson paused *Big Momma's House 2* and climbed clumsily out of her seat, her enormous and perfect breasts brushing the face of the old lady in the seat next to her. The old lady didn't seem to mind, and Dr Amyson wouldn't have minded if she'd reciprocated either...

For goodness sake, she thought to herself in her

mind. She was so deprived of incredibly incredible sex that she was now considering inviting a lady old enough to be her grandma to join her in the toilets...

Well, thought Dr Amyson, *if she had false teeth, she'd be good at licking her pussy like a dog licking the filling out of an Oreo...*

No, Dr Amyson, stop, she told herself. So, she removed her amazing breasts from the old lady's face and went to the toilet. Thankfully there was no queue, so she went straight in and sat down.

She didn't even need to go to the toilet; Dr Amyson just needed a change of scenery. The flight from Finland to North Virginia was a long one, and she was already on her third re-watch of *Big Momma's House 2*.

She breathed in and let out a long, exasperated sigh.

If only it was the long sigh of satisfaction that usually followed sex.

There was a knock at the door.

'Just a minute,' she said.

There was another knock.

'I'll be done in a second,' she said louder.

A third knock rapped on the door.

'One minute; I'm nearly done,' she said louderer.

Then a fourth knock.

Dr Amyson huffed. Why was this person being so impatient? They couldn't have needed to poo that badly; if they did, they'd have visited one of the other numerous toilets onboard the aircraft.

Dr Amyson unlocked the door and it concertinaed open like an accordion.

Dr Amyson gasped.

She felt a tingle in her vagina, like she had just

dipped it in vinegar.

Standing there was the air hostess in the burgundy skirt. She had a tiny, upturned smile, like a schoolgirl who knew she was doing something naughty, like using a calculator in an algebra test. But, as she stood there, her breasts quaking due to mild turbulence, Dr Amyson knew. Oh, she knew.

'You seem a little stressed, mon cherry,' said the air hostess in a seductively alluring French accent.

'Yes,' said Dr Amyson, taken aback by the air hostesses' hotness. Her bottom was delectable.

'I can 'elp you wiz zat,' she said, slowly licking her lip like she'd just devoured a chicken wing.

'In here?' asked Dr Amyson.

'Wee wee,' said the air hostess, closing and locking the bathroom door. Her nipples poked through her air hostess blouse like she had brought in two extra peanuts, which Dr Amyson couldn't wait to masticate.

Suddenly, without warning, shockingly, the air hostess dove vagina-first towards Dr Amyson, and the two locked themselves in an embrace tighter than a Yorkshireman haggling at a car boot sale. First their lips entangled, their tongues combating one another, giving off just a slight tingle like electric eels battling for dominance inside a smooth, pink cave. Dr Amyson felt her breasts inflate with anticipation as she snatched at her counterpart's boobies, which were equally as impressive.

Dr Amyson tore at the air hostesses' blouse, the buttons twanging off in every direction and shattering the tiny airplane bathroom mirror. She buried her face between her titties, which were big and soft like ripened wheels of cheese. She could barely breathe, they were so nice.

Then it was the air hostesses' turn. She pulled Dr Amyson up with such animalistic, lusty ferocity that she sat on the back of the toilet, at perfect height for Dr Amyson's knockers to be suckled like a vacuum cleaner on the highest setting. Pleasure so good it was like she was being stabbed by a thousand hot knives that coursed across Dr Amyson's skin, from her supple, brownish areola, right down to her pink surprise, which was her nickname for her vagina.

The air hostess must have sensed what Dr Amyson was feeling, because before she even knew what was happening, the French vixen was Frenching her pussy, her tongue lapping at her vertical lips like it was an ice pop melting on a hot summer's day.

Things went all blurry for a moment.

Her eyes crossed.

Explosions crackled all around her—was she

dying?

No. She was *living*.

These sounds were inside her head — nay — they were inside her vagina, because, in that moment, Dr Amyson experienced the most intense pleasuregasm any human being or animal had ever sensationalised. It was like an entire football stadium's worth of excited fans had stomped down on her pink surprise until she had to clench her teeth and scream. Scream. SCREAM!

Scream.

'Wow,' said Dr Amyson, brushing her beautiful and lovely hair out of her face.

'Your vagina is very tasty,' the air hostess said in her French accent.

'Thank you,' said Dr Amyson.

She couldn't believe it. An earth-shattering (or, because she was in a plane, sky-shattering) orgasm that made her, for one brief moment, consider asking this woman to be her wife.

The French beauty obviously felt the same. She took out a mascara pen and wrote her email address, *bustyfrenchbeauty69@gmail.com,* right across Dr Amyson's buttery breasts.

Then Dr Amyson went back to her seat with a smile on her face and a skip in her vagina. She watched another ten minutes of *Big Momma's House 2.* She laughed. She was relaxed.

Until, that is, she got a text…

Oh no. Oh no, Dr Amyson, oh no.

The text said: *Your Covid test results are in – positive. Please maintain social distancing. Goodbye.*

Dr Amyson's heart began to beat faster than a drummer beating really fast.

What had she done?

What… had… she… done…

End of flashback

Several moments of sheer intense pleasure, followed by eleven and a half hours of worry. Immediately after receiving the text, Dr Amyson had done everything she could to further prevent any possible spread. Did she have the dick strain of the virus? She was fully vaccinated, so that must have been it. She must have been infected with the dick strain at the microbiology convention.

Damn those microbiologists!

If it was true, if she did have the dick strain, then she would be the first person in America with a confirmed case. The press would eat her alive, more than the air hostess had eaten her vagina alive.

Microbiologist is a super spreader of new COVID-19 variant, they would say.

Then her career would be over and she'd be fired from her job at the lab and she would never get to go to the annual Finnish microbiology convention ever again! Imagine all the sex she would miss out on!

Despite it being the early hours of the morning, the lab canteen door opened, and the sexy young intern strutted into the room. She had big tits that could barely be contained within her lab outfit and plump lips that glistened like a droplet of water glistening in the desert sun.

Dr Amyson gasped. She covered her mouth and ran from the canteen, whilst the intern called after asking her if she was okay.

But Dr Amyson wasn't okay. If she was honest with herself, she felt absolutely fine, which meant she must have been asymptomatic, which is the word microbiologists use for people who are ill but feel fine.

Dr Amyson had no choice. She had to find out if she was carrying the dick strain. If she was, she would go home and immediately self-isolate. It was a race against the clock.

It wasn't in her department, but her lab had access to a COVID-19 test machine which was in room 7B. Dr Amyson snuck down the corridor to room 7B, then gently opened the door, gently closed the door, and gently switched on the light. There was only an hour until the COVID-19 team would start work, so Dr Amyson knew she had to act fast and gently.

She pressed the 'on' button on the COVID-19 machine and it thrummed to life in a similar way to how her vagina awakened at the thought of big tits smushed against her face like the intern's in the canteen…

NO, Dr Amyson yelled at herself in her head.

She couldn't think about the intern's incredible boobs yet; she had to figure out if she was carrying the dick strain of COVID-19!

Dr Amyson swabbed the back of her throat with a swab, then swabbed the swab up her nose, before placing the swab in the swab reader on the COVID-19 machine. She punched in a bunch of numbers she knew, then the COVID-19 machine began to groan and squirm and thud as it read the swab sample.

DING.

Dr Amyson held her breath as she leaned in close to the screen to read what it said. She was terrified. She was panicked. She was.

She was…

Negative.

Sure, she had COVID-19, but she didn't have the dick strain.

Thank you Billymungus!

She no longer had to worry about being a super spreader.

She wouldn't be the one to bring the dick strain to America.

She couldn't... she...

What was that?

She leaned in closer to the screen. It said, *New variant found: VG1NA.*

Wait... what?

Another new variant?

And she was patient number one?

HOLY BILLYMUNGUS.

Dr Amyson ran from the COVID-19 lab to her office, where she threw herself down into her comfy office chair and, after reading the email address again that had been written across her incredible breasts, she sent an email to the sexy air hostess:

Hello, my beautiful,

Thank you for that wonderful sex today, however I come bearing news.

Please self-isolate. I have been found to be carrying a brand-new variant of the Coronavirus known as VG1NA.

Please tell your local authorities.

I'm sorry, my princess.

Dr Amyson x

Amy sat back in her chair. What was this new variant found for the first time in herself? Had she caught it at the microbiology convention? Would it be resistant to vaccines, like the dick strain, or was it less severe? Was it *more* severe?

Dr Amyson's computer blinked. The sexy air hostess had responded.

Mon Cherry,

Wee, I ave also been diagnosed wiz ze Coronavirus.

I haz ze dick strain.

All my love.

Air hostess

Dr Amyson stared at the screen.

She stared and stared and stared.

What did this mean?

WHAT DID THIS MEAN?

Suddenly, her vagina twinged like she'd been stung by a lustful scorpion. Her breasts thundered together like boulders clashing under a crescent moon. Her bottom puckered and a ripple of intense pain and pleasure echoed throughout her body in a cataclysm of erogenous persuasion she couldn't even describe. Her feet hurt.

Dr Amyson began to run.

She didn't know why. She didn't know where

she was going.

She just ran.

And ran.

Until —

'Dr Amyson, hello,' said the sexual intern.

'Hi,' said Dr Amyson, sweat pouring from her face like she'd just enjoyed a marathon sex session.

Sex...

'You seem flustered; is there anything I can help you with?'

Dr Amyson clung to the wall like a gecko.

Her vision blurred and her vagina pulsated like it had a heartbeat of her own.

'Dr Amyson?' uttered the sexy intern.

'UNGH,' groaned Dr Amyson.

'What's wrong?' she asked, open-mouthed.

Dr Amyson fell to the floor clutching her big,

beautiful chest. Every muscle in her body ached, but especially her vagina. Her heart beat and her head span like she'd been riding a rollercoaster type ride in the dark.

And then, like a light bulb had sprung to life in her grey matter, she realised what was happening. Being a microbiologist, Dr Amyson had studied the work of Dr Gurtlychund and Dr Alexa Ashingtonford and Dr Kelly. She knew what had happened to them. What turmoil and sex they had experienced.

How the virus had caused them to change. To mutate...

And it was happening to her now, too.

The dick strain she had clearly caught from the buxom air hostess aboard the 2:52 flight from Finland to North Virginia was merging inside her body with the VG1NA strain, the... vagina strain.

The two strains were combining inside her body, rocketing from her genitals to her brain and back again, splicing her cells with the virus, changing her very being from human to… something else.

The intern screamed a terrified scream as Dr Amyson's skin transformed into a deep, crimson shade of red. Tiny bumps grew from her skin—which Dr Amyson instantly recognised as protein spikes—she had never seen them so clearly before. So closely. So… sexy...

Her lab top burst open, her boobies now so big, so red, that just glancing at them was like staring into the centre of the sun. It was a glorious, yet intoxicating sight. And the intern had fallen into their spell.

But her vagina. Oh, her vagina.

It was lean and muscular, like a thicc slab of freshly butchered, high-quality meat hanging in an abattoir window. It oozed pleasure fluid, which the sexy intern couldn't resist. She dropped to her knees and began slurping at it like she'd been shipwrecked on an island for weeks and Dr Amyson's vagina was a delicious glass of Pepsi.

Power coursed through Dr Amyson's veins. She felt like she could take on an entire army — both strength-wise, and sexually. As the intern gnawed at her pussy flaps, she made sounds that Dr Amyson had never heard before. Sounds of hunger. Of pleasure.

Sounds she hadn't even heard at the microbiology convention.

Dr Amyson grabbed the intern by the waist and pulled her up until their eyes met. At first, the intern looked taken aback. Maybe even a little scared. But then slowly, gently, carefully, their lips met. Dr Amyson felt the intern's tongue investigate the inside of her mouth, further than any tongue had ever explored. She returned the favour, her own tongue now comparable to a hairless ferret, snaking its way down the intern's throat which she seemed to like a little bit.

Then, the intern suckled at Dr Amyson's massive tits. It felt great, and she let her do it for fifteen minutes before returning the favour. Somehow, and this had never happened to her before, but Dr Amyson orgasmed with a nipple between her teeth. It was certainly a day for new experiences.

Power flowed through Dr Amyson's body like she was the Hoover dam and the lust was the Colorado River. She held the intern in her hands, now tiny like a tiny doll with tiny arms and tiny legs compared to her own — which were not tiny. Just the thought of the power that pulsed through her was enough to bring her to a sticky climax, vaginal fluid erupting from her vagina like it were an Icelandic volcano.

But it was only a taster of the orgasm she knew she was capable of.

Dr Amyson and the intern scissored right there on the floor. They rubbed their vaginas together and moaned and it felt incredible, even better than the time she watched porn with her ex-mother-in-law.

It was insane. Dr Amyson had no words to describe what had happened or how it had happened. It had just happened. It. Happened.

An orgasm slammed Dr Amyson in the ovaries like she'd been shot at with a machine gun. **RA TA TA TA TA!** Except it wasn't bullets she was being shot with, it was pleasure, over and over and over until she made a roar so loud and grunty it shook the windows like an earthquake had shifted the very foundations of the building.

Except it wasn't an earthquake. It was a pleasurequake.

The floor was sodden with juices that had been expelled from their two bodies, from every which orifice (hole) the two of them had. It didn't matter. It was proof that they had just encountered a sexual release that was unrivalled. Besides, the cleaners would start their shift in twenty minutes, and they'd clean it up so nobody would slip on it.

But what did this mean for Dr Amyson?

She shook hands with the intern and she left the lab, both of them with big, broad smiles on their faces, bigger than all four of their tits combined.

Where would she go now?

What would she do?

She was outside the lab.

She was a new strain. Clearly, the vaccine could

not contain it.

But could she contain herself?

She had her doubts.

She was here to stay.

About the Author

M.J. Edwards is a writer, board game enthusiast and trainee exhibitionist. *Kissing the Coronavirus 3: The Mutant Strain,* came to her in a fever dream after accidentally dropping some of her ferret's worm medication in her glass of rosé

She is currently on dating app Tinder looking for the next love of her life. Despite three awkward dates, a one-night stand, and a man who spoke through sock puppets, she is yet to give up hope.

For now, her love for writing will do.

Follow her on Twitter @MJEdwardsAuthor

Made in the USA
Coppell, TX
19 July 2021

59186228R10022